CH

SCOOBY-DOO!
READ ALL ABOUT IT!

LIKE, I *DON'T* WANT TO BELIEVE!

PAUL KUPPERBERG
WRITER

FABIO LAGUNA
ARTIST

TRAVIS LANHAM
LETTERER

HEROIC AGE
COLORIST

HARVEY RICHARDS
EDITOR

COVER BY VINCENT DEPORTER

Spotlight

visit us at www.abdopublishing.com

Reinforced library bound edition published in 2013 by Spotlight, a division of the ABDO Group, PO Box 398166, Minneapolis, MN 55439. Spotlight produces high-quality reinforced library bound editions for schools and libraries. Published by agreement with Warner Bros.-A Time Warner Company.

Printed in the United States of America, North Mankato, Minnesota.
102012
012013
♻This book contains at least 10% recycled materials.

Library of Congress Cataloging-in-Publication Data

Kupperberg, Paul.
 Scooby-Doo in Read all about it! / writer, Paul Kupperberg ; artist, Fabio Laguna. -- Reinforced library bound edition.
     pages cm. -- (Scooby-Doo graphic novels)
  ISBN 978-1-61479-053-2
 1. Graphic novels. I. Laguna, Fabio, illustrator. II. Scooby-Doo (Television program) III. Title. IV. Title: Read all about it!
 PZ7.7.K87Scl 2013
 741.5'973--dc23
                          2012033327

All Spotlight books are reinforced library bindings
and manufactured in the United States of America.

SCOOBY-DOO!

Table of Contents

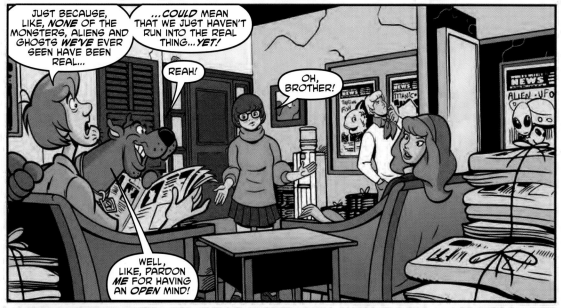

SHAGGY: JUST BECAUSE, LIKE, *NONE* OF THE MONSTERS, ALIENS AND GHOSTS *WE'VE* EVER SEEN HAVE BEEN REAL...

SHAGGY: ...*COULD* MEAN THAT WE JUST HAVEN'T RUN INTO THE REAL THING...*YET!*

SCOOBY: REAH!

DAPHNE: OH, BROTHER!

SHAGGY: WELL, LIKE, PARDON *ME* FOR HAVING AN *OPEN* MIND!

VELMA: "BIGFOOT'S SHOPPING SECRETS"...*NOBODY'S* MIND IS OPEN *ENOUGH* TO BELIEVE THAT!

WORLD'S WEEKLY NEWS — "BIG FOOT'S SHOPPING SECRETS TO SAVE $$!"

WORLD'S WEEKLY NEWS — DOGGIE CASINO TO OPEN IN LAS VEGAS!"

VELMA: I WONDER WHY THE PUBLISHER WANTS TO MEET WITH US...? HE *MUST* KNOW WE DON'T BELIEVE *ANY* OF THIS NONSENSE!

TRUSDALE: ...TO HAVE THE MOST INCREDIBLE STORY OF THE 21ST CENTURY *VERIFIED* BY AMERICA'S MOST *FAMOUS* MYTH BUSTERS!

FRED: HI, YOU MUST BE MR. *TRUSDALE!*

TRUSDALE: EVERETT T. TRUSDALE, AT YOUR SERVICE!

TRUSDALE: WHICH IS *EXACTLY* WHY I NEED THE SERVICES OF *MYSTERY, INC...*

FRED: NO DISRESPECT MEANT, SIR, BUT *MOST* OF THE STORIES IN YOUR PAPER ARE SORT OF RIDICULOUS AND...

TRUSDALE: HAH! *THAT'S* WHERE YOU'RE *WRONG,* FRED...

...ALL THE STORIES ARE RIDICULOUS... BECAUSE *ALL* OF THEM ARE *MADE UP* BY OUR WRITERS!

HUH?! THEN WHAT DO YOU WANT *US* FOR...?

WE'VE UNCOVERED A *REAL* STORY THAT'S SO *INCREDIBLE*, IT WILL *ROCK* THE WORLD...

...BUT *NOBODY* WILL BELIEVE IT IF *WE* REPORT IT!

BUT IF *MYSTERY, INC.* CAN PROVE IT'S *TRUE*, THEN THE WORLD WILL BE *FORCED* TO ACCEPT IT...

HOLY SMOKE!

ROW!

NO ONE KNOWS WHERE THE ALIEN IS...

...THAT AN *ALIEN SPACECRAFT* WAS FOUND CRASHED IN THE DEEP FORESTS! THE MILITARY'S TAKEN IT TO A SECRET LOCATION--

--BUT THE SHIP'S *PILOT* STILL HAS *NOT* BEEN FOUND! THERE'S A MASSIVE MILITARY *MANHUNT* GOING ON FOR IT, ER...HIM!

SOON...

MR. TRUSDALE SAID YOU, LIKE, KNEW *WHERE* TO FIND THE ALIEN. IS HE HERE?

WELL, THAT'S NOT *EXACTLY* TRUE, SHAGGY...

...BUT I KNOW PEOPLE WHO CAN TELL ME WHERE TO FIND THE PEOPLE WHO *DO* KNOW WHERE THE ALIEN IS!

ARE YOU *SURE* ABOUT THIS, SIR?

IT'S BEEN A WHILE SINCE I DID ANY *REAL* REPORTING, BUT... YES! I *TRUST* THESE PEOPLE.

BUZZ

BUZZ

WELL, WE'VE COME *THIS* FAR...!

DAVE... YOU'RE *LATE!* WE WERE GETTING *WORRIED...!*

SORRY, BUT WE RAN INTO SOME, ER... *TRAFFIC!* RYAN AND *DEB TRAINOR,* THESE ARE THE PEOPLE I TOLD YOU ABOUT!

MR. SEGAL SAYS YOU KNOW SOMETHING ABOUT THE *ALIEN...?*

YEAH, DO WE *EVER!* THE BLASTED THING ALMOST *KILLED* US!

OH, IT WASN'T LIKE THAT AT *ALL,* RYAN! WE WERE *CAMPING* IN THE FOREST THE OTHER NIGHT...

"...AND WE HAD JUST GOTTEN INTO OUR TENT TO GO TO SLEEP--"

WARREN *DID* FOLLOW WHATEVER WAS OUT THERE... HE KNOWS WHERE IT WENT TO *HIDE*...

IF HE'LL LEAD US THERE, WE'LL *HAVE* OUR PROOF! THANKS!

HEY, YOU KIDS... STOP!

≥Gulp!≤ HE'S COMING *FAST*, YOU GUYS...!

THIS SHOULD SLOW HIM DOWN!

I ORDER YOU TO... ≥OOOFF!≤

THUDD

MOMENTS LATER...

THANK GOODNESS I HAD MY CELLPHONE WITH ME! LET'S SEE, WARREN WALLACE LIVES CLOSE BY...

...I'M GETTING G.P.S. DIRECTIONS NOW! HE DOESN'T SEEM TO BE INVOLVED WITH ANY U.F.O. GROUPS... HMM!

THIS IS THE ADDRESS!

AND THAT'S GOT TO, LIKE, BE OUR MAN!

YOU MUST BE MR. SEGAL, THE REPORTER! RYAN CALLED TO TELL ME YOU WERE ON YOUR WAY!

I NEED YOUR *HELP*, MR. WALLACE! RYAN SAYS YOU *KNOW* WHERE THE ALIEN IS...!?

I THINK SO! YOU CAN FOLLOW ME... BUT WE'D BETTER HURRY! HE *ALSO* SAID THE ARMY'S ON ITS WAY!

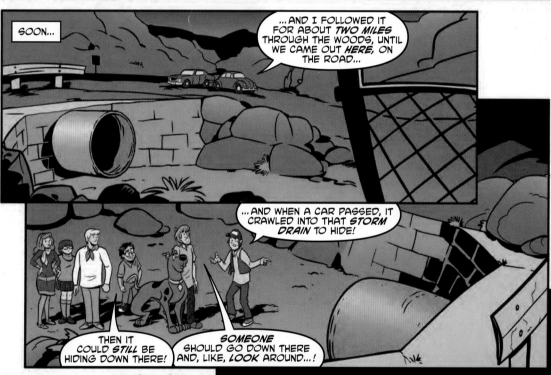

SOON...

...AND I FOLLOWED IT FOR ABOUT *TWO MILES* THROUGH THE WOODS, UNTIL WE CAME OUT *HERE*, ON THE ROAD...

...AND WHEN A CAR PASSED, IT CRAWLED INTO THAT *STORM DRAIN* TO HIDE!

THEN IT COULD *STILL* BE HIDING DOWN THERE!

SOMEONE SHOULD GO DOWN THERE AND, LIKE, *LOOK* AROUND...!

YEAH! *THANKS* FOR VOLUNTEERING!!

HUH?! BUT... I *DIDN'T...?!*

...I GOTTA LEARN TO KEEP MY MOUTH *SHUT...*

≶Ulp!≶

DO YOU *SEE* ANYTHING, SHAGGY?

ALL I CAN SEE IS *MY LIFE,* LIKE, FLASHING BEFORE MY EYES! IF...IF THE ALIEN *HAD* BEEN HERE, I THINK HE'S...

...HE'S... HE'S...HE'S...

...HE'S *DOWN THERE!!*

LIKE... ≶*OOOFFF!*≶

PAMPFF

WHAMM

I *KNEW* IF I STAYED *OUT OF SIGHT,* YOU'D LEAD ME TO... HUH?!

EMPTY...?! ARE YOU *SURE* YOU SAW SOMETHING, SHAGGY?

THAT *FLASH* WAS THE ALIEN BEING *TELEPORTED* TO SAFETY! *BLAST!* WE *ALMOST...!*

≶*sniff! sniff!*≶ WAIT...THAT *ODOR!* IT'S ALUMINUM POWDER AND POTASSIUM PERCHLORATE...*MAGICIAN'S FLASH POWDER!*

AND YOU KNOW SOMETHING *ELSE...?*

IS SOMEONE THERE?

SHUFF

CLICK

SHUFF

I SAID, "IS ANYONE..."

≶Gasp!≶

HOMINA-HOMINA-HOMINA-HOMINA...

THE MISSING MUMMY MYSTERY

WRITER: *JOHN ROZUM*   ARTIST: *SCOTT NEELY*   COLORIST: *HEROIC AGE*
LETTERER: *TRAVIS LANHAM*   EDITOR: *HARVEY RICHARDS*

WHAT *IS IT,* MAN?

GET AHOLD OF YOURSELF, DAVID, AND TELL ME WHAT'S WRONG.

HE-HE-HE HE...

HE-HE-HE. HE WENT FOR A LITTLE WALK.

≥Gasp!≤

HE-HE-HE-HE-HE-HE...

THEN WHAT HAPPENED, SIR WEMPLE?

AFTER THE POLICE ARRIVED I SENT MR. MANNERS--THE NIGHT GUARD--HOME. I TOLD HIM TO TAKE A VACATION, BUT HE REFUSED. HE SAID HE WOULDN'T HEAR OF IT.

BUT *WHY?* IT SURE SOUNDS LIKE HE COULD USE ONE. POOR MAN.

WELL, THE WAY I LOOK AT IT IS THAT IF THE *LIVING MUMMY* IS SOMEWHERE *OUTSIDE* OF THE MUSEUM, THEN I'D RATHER BE *HERE INSIDE*, WHERE THE MUMMY *ISN'T*.

LIKE, *NOT US.* I COUNT *FIVE* UNOPENED SARCOPHOGUSUMUSSES WHICH MEANS THE MUMMY HAS FIVE FRIENDS WHO MIGHT DECIDE THEY NEED SOME EXERCISE, TOO.

I'D MUCH RATHER BE *OUTSIDE* THE MUSEUM THAN *IN*.

RHEE TROO.

GREAT IDEA!

RHIT IS?

YOU TWO GO OUTSIDE AND SEE IF ANYONE HAS SEEN ANYTHING. ASK AROUND.

A WALKING MUMMY IS SURE TO HAVE ATTRACTED SOMEONE'S ATTENTION, OR AT LEAST HAVE LEFT SOME CLUES BEHIND.

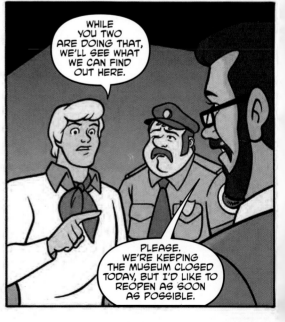

WHILE YOU TWO ARE DOING THAT, WE'LL SEE WHAT WE CAN FIND OUT HERE.

PLEASE. WE'RE KEEPING THE MUSEUM CLOSED TODAY, BUT I'D LIKE TO REOPEN AS SOON AS POSSIBLE.

MR. MANNERS, WOULD YOU MIND WALKING US THROUGH YOUR EVENING, LEADING UP TO YOUR SIGHTING OF THE WALKING MUMMY?

WELL, LET'S SEE. I ARRIVED AT 11:45 LAST NIGHT, LIKE I ALWAYS DO, TO START THE NIGHT SHIFT.

"AFTER I CHANGED INTO MY UNIFORM, I WENT TO THE GUARD STATION TO RELIEVE STEVE BANNING--HE'S THE GUARD WHO WORKS THE SHIFT BEFORE MINE."

HOW'S IT BEEN, STEVE?

QUIET AS A TOMB, DAVID. JUST LIKE ALWAYS.

"I TOOK MY PLACE BEHIND THE DESK, AND CHECKED THE MONITORS. THE ONLY MOVEMENT ON ANY OF THEM WAS STEVE WALKING TO THE LOCKER ROOM. AFTER A FEW MINUTES, I GOT UP AND BEGAN MY ROUNDS."

IT USUALLY TAKES ABOUT FORTY MINUTES TO COMPLETE MY ROUNDS. NOTHING WAS OUT OF THE ORDINARY UNTIL I ENTERED THE EGYPTIAN WING ABOUT HALF AN HOUR INTO MY ROUNDS. I NEVER FINISHED THEM.

CAN YOU PLAY BACK A RECORDING OF THE TIME THAT YOU REACHED THE EGYPTIAN WING?

NO. THIS IS AN OLD SECURITY SYSTEM. WE ONLY RECORD IF WE SEE ANYTHING UNUSUAL WHILE WE ARE IN THIS ROOM.

WHAT WERE YOU DOING IN THE MUSEUM SO LATE?

I OFTEN WORK LATE AT NIGHT. WHEN THE MUSEUM IS FULLY STAFFED DURING THE DAY, I'M OFTEN INTERRUPTED BY PHONE CALLS AND QUESTIONS FROM OTHER STAFF MEMBERS THAT THE SCHOLARLY ASPECT OF MY WORK HERE FALLS BY THE WAYSIDE.

DID YOU SEE THE WALKING MUMMY?

NO, SIR. I DID NOT. I WAS ALERTED BY THE SOUND OF MR. MANNERS'S CRIES. I WENT TO INVESTIGATE. MY FIRST IMPRESSION IS THAT HE'D BEEN INJURED.

I WONDER HOW SHAGGY AND SCOOBY ARE DOING?

THIS IS THE LOCKER ROOM, THOUGH I'M NOT SURE WHAT YOU HOPE TO FIND HERE.

DOES ANYONE ELSE USE IT BESIDES THE *GUARDS?*

NO.

AND CAN YOU OPEN *ALL* OF THESE LOCKERS?

YES. THE *KEYS* ARE IN THE GUARD ROOM.

LET'S GO GET THEM.

SO, YOU LOST YOUR MOMMY AT THE MUSEUM?

NO, IT WAS ALREADY GONE BY THE TIME WE GOT THERE.

DOES YOUR MOMMY WORK AT THE MUSEUM?

...

YOU COULD SAY THAT.

AHA! *NOW* WE'RE GETTING SOMEWHERE.

NOW, WHAT'S YOUR MOMMY'S NAME?

THEY'RE GONE!

MR. MANNERS, WILL YOU OPEN THAT LOCKER, PLEASE?

MR. MANNERS, WHO IS IN THE MUSEUM NOW BESIDES YOURSELF, ME AND MY FRIENDS, AND SIR WEMPLE?

NO ONE. WE'RE CLOSED.

I BET I KNOW WHOSE LOCKER THAT IS.

FREDDIE, TAKE A LOOK AT THE MONITORS AND TELL ME IF YOU SEE ANYONE BESIDES US.

IT'S THE MUMMY! HE'S MOVING THROUGH THE DINOSAUR HALL!

HE'S TAKING AN ELEVATOR DOWN TO THE EGYPTIAN WING.

QUICK! FOLLOW ME.

I KNOW WHERE WE CAN CUT HIM OFF.

DO EITHER OF YOU KNOW ANCIENT EGYPTIAN FOR "HALT! YOU'RE UNDER ARREST"?

!

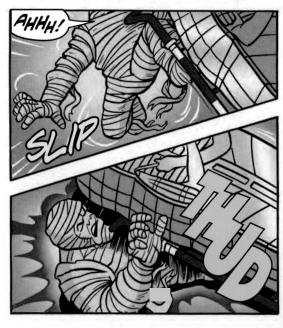

AHHH!

SLIP

THUD

EXCUSE ME, BUT THESE TWO ARE LOOKING FOR THEIR MOMMY.

RIGHT HERE, OFFICER. ONLY I THINK THIS MUMMY WILL BE ACCOMPANYING YOU BACK TO THE POLICE STATION.

STEVE BANNING!

JUST AS I EXPECTED.

WHEN MR. MANNERS AND I FIRST VISITED THE LOCKER ROOM, I NOTICED A STRIP OF *GAUZE BANDAGE* STICKING OUT OF ONE OF THE LOCKERS, AS WELL AS A *DOLLY* FOR MOVING BOXES WHICH HAD NO BUSINESS BEING THERE.

THEN I STARTED PIECING EVENTS TOGETHER.

BANNING HAD HIS CRIME PLANNED WELL. BEING A GUARD, HE HAD ACCESS TO *EVERYTHING.* HE ALSO KNEW THE ROUTINES OF THE GUARDS. WHEN MR. MANNERS RELIEVED HIM OF DUTY, HE NEVER WENT HOME.

HE KNEW THAT MANNERS WOULD BEGIN HIS *ROUNDS* WHILE HE WAS IN THE *LOCKER ROOM,* GIVING HIM PLENTY OF TIME TO CHANGE INTO THE *MUMMY COSTUME* AND TO STATION HIMSELF IN THE EGYPTIAN WING WHERE HE PRETENDED TO COME TO LIFE AND LEAVE.

HE *STOLE* AND HID THE *REAL MUMMY* DURING HIS OWN SHIFT, I'M GUESSING TO SELL TO A PRIVATE COLLECTOR. HE THOUGHT HE'D BE MORE LIKELY TO GET AWAY WITH IT IF PEOPLE THOUGHT THE MUMMY LEFT ON ITS OWN.

CLEARLY THE PERSON HE WAS DEALING WITH WANTED THE *SARCOPHAGUS* TOO, FORCING HIM TO COME BACK TO GET IT.

DO YOU HAVE ANYTHING YOU'D LIKE TO SAY BEFORE I PLACE YOU UNDER ARREST?

I WANT MY MOMMY!

THE END